Written & created by Jessica Parkin
(info@jessicaparkin.co.uk)

Illustrated by Phillip Reed
(info@phillipreed.net)

Granny's Cat

Written & created by Jessica Parkin

Illustrated by Phillip Reed

This is
Charlie

This is
Daddy

This is
Mummy

This is
Me (Tilly)

This is
Granny Vi

This is
Grandpa Joe

This is
Marmaduke

I love Marmaduke.

Marmaduke always runs away
when I try to stroke him.

One day I crept up and tried to stroke him while he was sitting down.

Marmaduke scratched my arm and made me cry.

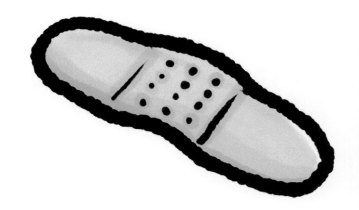

My arm hurt and I cried a lot. Grandpa Joe gave me a cuddle to make me feel better.

Grandpa Joe told me
Marmaduke was a shy cat.
He suggested we
should go together.

Marmaduke did not see us creeping into the room.

Grandpa Joe picked up Marmaduke and put him on his lap while I waited behind the sofa.

When Marmaduke fell asleep,
Grandpa Joe let me stroke him.
Marmaduke woke up but
he did not run away.

I was happy and I went to tell Granny Vi. She gave me a nice cake to eat.

I still can't catch Marmaduke.
I hope Grandpa Joe will help
me again next time I visit.

Other books in the Tilly Tales series:

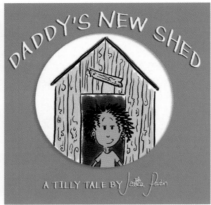

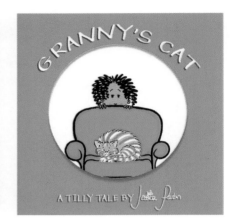

Scan me for website

Printed in Great Britain
by Amazon

50115593R00018